# IF IT WEREN'T FOR YOU

by **Charlotte Zolotow**

pictures by **G. Brian Karas**

**HarperCollins**Publishers

If It Weren't for You

Library of Congress Cataloging-in-Publication Data
Zolotow, Charlotte, date
    If it weren't for you / by Charlotte Zolotow ; pictures by G. Brian Karas. — 1st ed.
        p.    cm.
    Summary: An older sibling imagines the advantages of not having a younger sibling around,
but then thinks of one disadvantage.
    ISBN-10: 0-06-027875-7 (trade bdg.) — ISBN-13: 978-0-06-027875-5 (trade bdg.)
    ISBN-10: 0-06-027876-5 (lib. bdg.) — ISBN-13: 978-0-06-027876-2 (lib. bdg.)
    [1. Sisters—Fiction.] I. Karas, G. Brian, ill.  II. Title.  III. Title: If it were not for you.
PZ7.Z771f 2006
[E]—dc22                                                                                          2005017786
                                                                                                          CIP
                                                                                                          AC

Typography by Drew Willis
1  2  3  4  5  6  7  8  9  10
❖
First Edition

If it weren't for you,
I'd be the only child

**and I'd get all the presents.**

I could have the whole last slice of cake
and the biggest piece of candy in the box.

If it weren't for you,

I could come home from school the long way,

**and I could watch any program I wanted on TV**

and keep the light on
late at night to read in bed.

No one would know if it weren't for you.

# If it weren't for you,

I could have a room of my own.

I could carve the pumpkin the way I want—
frowning,

**and I could cry without anyone knowing**

and play in the tub as long as I wanted each night

and always be the one to sit in the front.

If it weren't for you,
the treehouse would be just mine,

the dog would be just mine too,
and I'd teach him tricks,

**and I could have the whole bottle of soda**

and the chair facing the window at the table,
and we wouldn't ever have mashed turnips.

If it weren't for you,
the house would be quiet when I'm reading,

**and no one would ever say I have to set an example,**

and I could swing too high,
and my paintbrushes would never be mashed,
and I could have my two-wheeler now
instead of waiting.

But it's also true,

I'd have to be alone with the grown-ups
if it weren't for you.